D0871398

AWN

The *Fastest* Tortoise in *Town*

To Sylvie, for providing the spark
HC

For Mom and Dad, who always believe in me
KO

CANDLEWICK PRESS

Text copyright © 2023 by Howard Calvert. Illustrations copyright © 2023 by Karen Obuhanych. All rights reserved. No part of this book may be reproduced, transmitted, or stored in an information retrieval system in any form or by any means, graphic, electronic, or mechanical, including photocopying, taping, and recording, without prior written permission from the publisher. First US edition 2023. First published by Walker Books Ltd. (UK) 2023. Library of Congress Catalog Card Number 2022936839. ISBN 978-1-5362-2835-9. This book was typeset in AnkeSans. The illustrations were done in mixed media. Candlewick Press, 99 Dover Street, Somerville, Massachusetts 02144. www.candlewick.com.
Printed in Heshan, Guangdong, China. 23 24 25 26 27 28 LEO 10 9 8 7 6 5 4 3 2 1

The Fastest Tortoise in Town

FUN RUN

Howard Calvert   illustrated by **Karen Obuhanych**

I've entered a running race.

What have I done?
Me, Barbara Hendricks,
just a regular leopard tortoise.

RACING.

Against other animals.

In seven days' time. THAT'S JUST ONE WEEK!

What do you think my chances of winning are?
I would say ZERO. No chance of taking home the trophy.
After all, I'm well known for being slow.

But somehow, my owner and best friend, Lorraine, believes in me.
"I've never seen a faster tortoise than you, Barbara Hendricks," she says.

Lorraine decides that I should do some training.
"Strengthen your muscles," she says. "Build your stamina."
I'm confused. I thought mussels lived in the ocean!

Lorraine begins to take me out for walks.
Every single day.

On Monday, we're overtaken
by an absentminded worm.

On Tuesday, by Lily, who
just learned to walk.

On Wednesday, by Lorraine's great-grandpa, on his way to feed the ducks.

On Thursday, by Arlo's remote-controlled brachiosaurus.

And on Friday, we're overtaken by Mr. Beaton's out-of-control robo vacuum cleaner.
That pushes me over the edge.
I can't do this. It's impossible!

But Lorraine tells me it's perfectly normal to be worried.
"Don't worry about what anyone else is doing.
Just run your own race. Let's rest and eat ice cream tomorrow."

Before I know it, it is Sunday. Race day.
It's definitely a stay-in-my-shell type of day.

No legs out. Head staying firmly in.
Then I hear Lorraine's voice.

"Barbara Hendricks, I know you can hear me.
You don't have to race today
if you don't want to.
But how will you know if all
this training was worth anything
if you stay in your shell?"

She's right.

"Just think of it as a walk," continues Lorraine.
"Our walk we do every day. Together."

She's got me.

So away we go, to the stadium.

I steal a glance at my competitors.
A slug, a snail, a slow loris, a sloth,
and Woody the grumpy walrus.
I turn even greener.
Look at them!

The best of the best,
the fastest animals
I've ever seen!

We line up at the start.
It takes all my tortoise powers to stop
me from popping back into my shell.

The mayor raises her megaphone.

"On your marks . . .

get set . . .

GO!"

I put one foot in front of the other.

Then do it again.

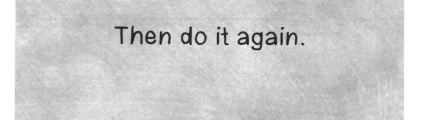

And again.

And again!

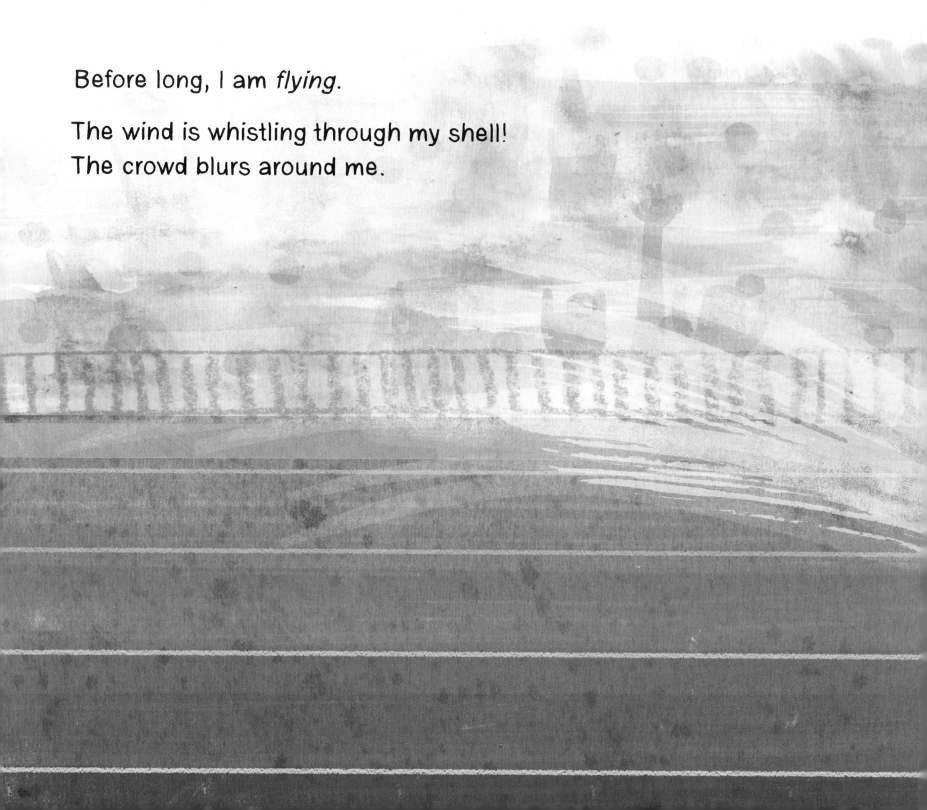

Before long, I am *flying*.

The wind is whistling through my shell!
The crowd blurs around me.

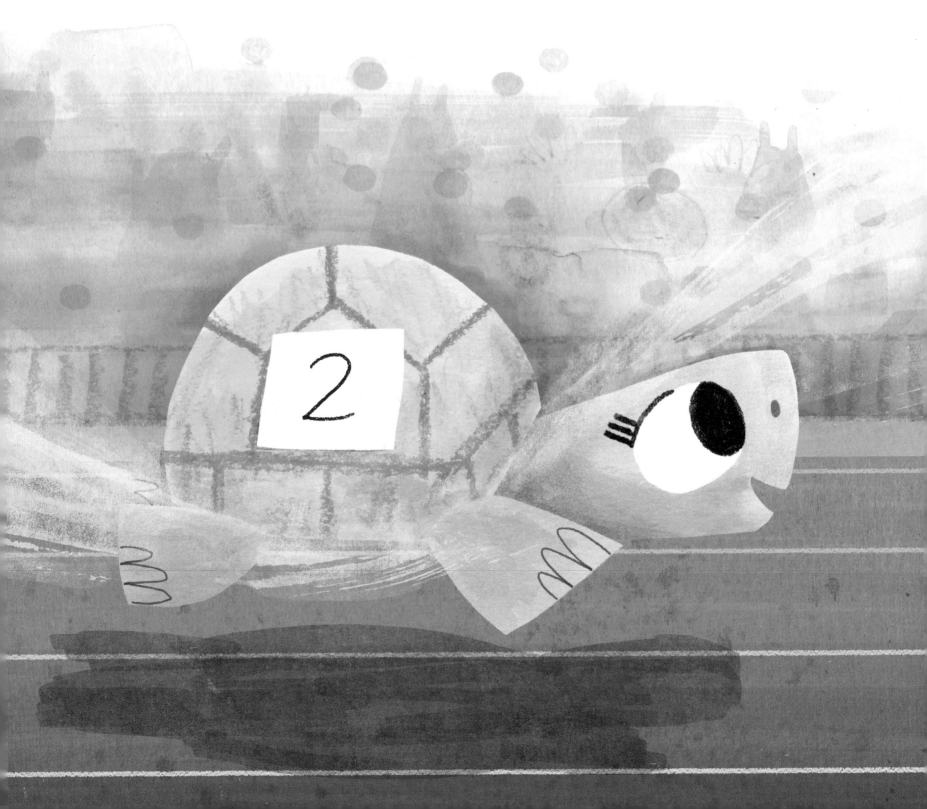

I stumble over the finish line.
I've done it! I finished! I raced!

The mayor has an announcement to make.
"The winner is . . . Barbara Hendricks!"

The crowd roars. It seems like a dream.
But it's real, and it feels magnificent!

As we leave, a hare bounds over.

"You're pretty fast
 for a tortoise," he says.
"Know what I think?
 I think we should race."

I peer up at Lorraine.
"Why not?" she says.

She's right.

After all, what do I have to lose?

31901069397547